To Martha,

I hope that you enjoy my book.

Love

Eliza Scott

x

The Adventures of Detective Dopeyworth

Elizabeth Green

Grosvenor House
Publishing Limited

This book is published by
Grosvenor House Publishing Ltd
Link House
140 The Broadway, Tolworth, Surrey, KT6 7HT.
www.grosvenorhousepublishing.co.uk

A CIP record for this book
is available from the British Library

ISBN 978-1-80381-222-9

Elizabeth Green was born and raised in Bolton, Lancashire but now resides in North Yorkshire with her husband, two dogs and two cats.

Elizabeth wrote the original version of Detective Dopeyworth when she was fourteen years old after receiving a typewriter for Christmas. Forty years later she found the forgotten story in her parents writing desk and, after a bit of a rewrite, she decided to share it with the world.

This book is dedicated to my wonderful Dad who loved Detective Dopeyworth and tucked him away safely until I was ready to share him with the world.

I love and miss you Dad.

It's better than a bacon buttie...and bacon butties are good.

I hope this makes you proud.

Acknowledgements

A huge thanks to the wonderful team that have worked alongside me to bring this book to publication. To my editor Eva Maria Dietrich Carreño, thank you for your patience, your enthusiasm and bringing out the best in me as a writer. I owe a huge debt of gratitude to my insanely talented illustrator Mike Cañas who has brought to life the characters that have lived in my head for so many years.

A massive thanks to the team at Grosvenor House Publishing for their support and guidance with particular praise to Julie and Dean for answering all of my ridiculous questions on a daily basis.

A huge thanks to my son Joe who never doubted I could do this and cheered me on all the way as well as supporting me massively with marketing and all of the stuff that he does so brilliantly.

Alan, thankyou for the many laughs. We got that bump on the head just right.

And finally to my Dad. Thank you. This one's for you.

Last Chance

"Now *just* you listen to me, Dopeyworth," boomed Mr Hart to the trembling figure who sat quivering before him. "Can't you see that you are not cut out to be a detective? You have got to be tough, strong and willing, like me. Not a snivelling little cloth head like yourself!"

Mr Hart slammed his huge fist down on the desk, making Jim, and the desk, tremble even further.

Malcolm Hart was a very scary boss even when he was in a good mood, and today, Jim could see beads of sweat glistening on his big bald head as he got angrier and angrier. He wore a very smart pin-striped suit that was slightly too tight around the middle. His trouser button looked like it was going to pop off at any second and hit Jim straight in the eye, but Jim kept his eyes firmly focused on Mr Hart's big, hairy, sausage-like fingers that were wagging furiously in his face.

"Okay, Dopeyworth." Mr Hart leaned forward, a little too close to Jim's face, and gave a very uninviting smile. "As I'm such a generous soul, I'm prepared to give you one, just one last chance. Today you will go out and solve a mystery... okay?"

"Yes, sir," Jim said but thought *Some flipping chance.*

James Augustus Dopeyworth didn't always come out on top in life. Poor Jim had never really found his way despite his best efforts. Every job he had ever been given ended in disaster no matter how hard he tried. He was always knocking things over and found himself in the unlikeliest of unfortunate situations. Nothing ever seemed to go right, and now he really was in trouble.

It hadn't always been this way. When Jim had been a little boy, he could do no wrong. With his mop of red curls and chubby cheeks, he was the apple of his mother's eye. He realised from a very early age that he wanted to be a good person. He wanted to help people. Helping people and being rewarded with a big smile, or even better, a big bar of chocolate, made Jim feel all warm inside. It was the best feeling in the world.

One Christmas morning, Jim had woken up to a huge sack full of presents that Santa had delivered to his house on Sherlockton Avenue, but his favourite gift was a Secret Spy box which contained an oversized magnifying glass and a fingerprint kit. Jim would spend hours scouring the house and garden looking for anything that went missing, and it was his absolute most favourite hobby. Every time he found a missing item (a sock or perhaps one of his mother's colourful earrings), his mum and dad would be so proud of him and reward him with a chocolate biscuit or a chocolate éclair. Jim loved it.

Over the years that followed, his mother bought Jim books about Sherlock Holmes, a full range of different sized magnifying glasses, even newspapers with holes in the middle. And the list went on and on. One day, she was sure, her James would become a national hero, just like his father. He was a natural. Jim, however, wasn't so sure he was cut out to be a detective despite it being all he had dreamed about. Maybe he would be better off being a postman. *But would Mother hear of it? No such thing.*

As Jim grew older, he never gave up on his dream of being a famous super sleuth, but his first job had been a little more down to earth: delivering the local newspaper.

"Good morning, Percy." Jim licked his lips as he walked through the door of the local bakery. "Here is the paper, and I will have one of your delicious éclairs to take away, please."

Percy Caramel ran the most prestigious confectioners in town and Jim loved dropping in with the newspaper. He sold the most scrumptious chocolate éclairs, Jim's favourite. They were just too gorgeous to resist!

There was quite a queue forming behind Jim, including a very tall man with greasy black hair. Jim was salivating over the thought of his mid-morning treat when he felt a sharp prod in his back. He turned around and inwardly groaned.

Oh no!!! It was Mrs Plumpton, his extremely nosey next-door neighbour.

"Well, if it isn't little chubby cheeks Jimmy," she boomed. "Ooh, you are starting to look just like your father." She stared pointedly at Jim's rather round tummy. "He used to like his cream cakes too."

Percy slid a large éclair hurriedly over the counter and Jim took a large bite to try and hide his embarrassment. It was easier not to engage in conversation.

"I remember when you were just this high," Mrs Plumpton continued. "Always peering around the garden with that huge magnifying glass, you were. I remember that time when you were so busy looking through it that you tripped over your dog and fell headfirst into the blackberry bush. Oh, it was so funny. You were always so clumsy... You didn't inherit your father's talents, did you?"

The whole bakery was listening on in amusement as Mrs Plumpton carried on.

"Oh and I will never forget that time you rushed out of the house with your belt undone and your trousers fell down!! Ha ha, we all got a good look at your underpants with yellow ducks on."

Poor Jim was getting redder by the minute. Percy looked on in sympathy and passed over another éclair while Jim just nodded and smiled, his cheeks full of cake like two big red balloons and sticky chocolate cream dripping down his chin.

"It's a shame really, isn't it?" Mrs Plumpton continued. "Ah well, at least you can deliver the papers."

Mrs Plumpton was really playing to her audience, particularly the very unattractive man with greasy black hair who was guffawing a little too loudly at Jim's misfortune.

Percy felt sorry for Jim. He knew that he wanted to be a detective and loved to catch up with him about all the latest goings on in town.

“Thanks very much, Mrs Plumpton.” Percy ushered the old lady out of the shop and turned his attention back to Jim, who was swallowing the last of his éclair and clutching his stomach.

“Have you heard about the latest robbery, Jim?” Percy slid another two éclairs over the counter. “They think it’s the Green Emerald Gang.”

“I have,” Jim replied. “Another big stash of jewels taken from poor Mrs Elvington. That’s the fourth one this month and they are still no closer to catching them.”

Jim grabbed the paper bag ready to leave.

“Thanks for the cakes, Percy. I will see you next week.” Jim turned quickly and bumped straight into the large man with greasy black hair who had been listening rather intently to the conversation.

“My pleasure, Jim. And mind the floor. I just mop—”

Too late. With one hand on the last chocolate éclair and the other in his newspaper satchel, Jim skidded on the wet tiles and landed, rather unceremoniously, on his bottom with his cake landing upside down on top of the head of the man who had been standing behind him.

“You idiot.”

Oops.

Percy helped Jim to his feet and assisted him in gathering up his scattered newspapers, but Jim only had eyes for the paper which had fallen open on the local job adverts page.

Trainee detective required. Apply within.

Not thinking twice, Jim tore the ad out of the paper.

“I must go,” he stuttered, holding the piece of paper tight to his chest. “Sorry about the mess, Percy.”

“Hey, you are forgetting your newspapers…’ Percy called after Jim, but Jim was already out of earshot.

Percy shook his head as he watched Jim race down the street. Every time he called in there was some kind of disaster or other.

Jim ran home as fast as he could after eating so many chocolate éclairs and, as soon as he got through the door at Sherlockton Avenue, he headed straight to his room. There was no time to waste. It was meant to be. He *had* to get that job.

Over the weeks that followed, Jim waited anxiously for the post to arrive each day, but there was never anything for him.

Every day he would listen to the letter box rattle with excitement, only to be disappointed moments later. Not even his beloved *Detective Monthly* magazine plopping onto the doormat could lift his spirits.

But one day everything changed.

"Jim, darling, there's a letter from Scotland Yard for you," his mother excitedly announced, waving a thick cream envelope under Jim's nose.

Jim held the letter in his hand for a moment and squeezed his eyes tight shut. He had all but given up hope as the days had ticked by.

"Open it then," his mother urged as Jim started to slowly peel the envelope back. His hands were shaking so much that he dropped the letter twice, and the second time it narrowly avoided dropping into his mug of tea.

He shook out the paper and began to read the words out loud.

Dear Mr Dopeyworth

Thank you for your recent application as trainee detective at Scotland Yard.

We are delighted to offer you a position as trainee and look forward to welcoming you...

"I'm in," he shrieked. "I'm a detective! I can't believe it!"

"Waaaahhhhhh," squealed Mrs Dopeyworth so loudly that Jim had to cover his ears with his hands. "Waaaahhhhhh. I'm so proud of you."

And so his adventure began.

***

"James Augustus Dopeyworth," the master of ceremonies had announced to the audience at his induction day. "Wear this badge with honour and pride and always uphold the values of the Detective Code."

"I will," whispered Jim as his mother looked on, bursting with pride. He had finally done it. He was a detective. This was the best moment of his life.

From that day onward, Mrs Dopeyworth decided that she would do whatever she could to help Jim, even if it meant she had to take charge. She was his mother.

She knew best. Whenever an obstacle appeared in his path she was always there with some comforting advice.

"Now, James," she would say over and over again, "you have got to reach up high for stardom. You must go through agony after agony to get to the top."

And this was precisely what Jim was thinking about as he left the office after his showdown with Mr Hart and set out for home with his head down. Agony after agony, that was certainly true. *Well, this time, I am not going to listen. I will come right out and tell her.*

He just wasn't good enough to be a detective. It was time to face reality. *I will never be a national hero*.

He was going to have to give up his dream and become a postman instead. A postman was a perfectly respectable job. He would still be helping people, and he had responsibilities now. There was Watson, his pet hamster, to think about.

"Nonsense, darling," his mother said when he told her. "You just sit down, and I'll make you a lovely mug of hot chocolate, and you will see the whole thing in a different light."

"But Mother," said Jim with a hint of desperation creeping into his voice. "You just don't understand. I'm no good at being a detective. My boss called me a cloth head and threatened to sack me if I didn't find a mystery to solve by today!"

"Oh darling," his mother sympathised. "It can't be that bad. Remember, to reach the top, you must go through agony after agony."

So you keep telling me, thought Jim. *I suppose I had better give it one more shot, and if it doesn't work this time, I will definitely stop*. Jim hated to disappoint his mother.

"Alright, Mother. I won't give up. You have always taught me that sometimes good things take time."

Mrs Dopeyworth beamed. "That's my little angel, now you drink up and go out there and find yourself a case to solve. I'll pack you up some of your favourite chocolate biscuits to keep your energy levels up."

So Jim was, once again, on the long road to becoming a hero. Finding a mystery to solve wasn't exactly easy. It seemed impossible, but he had to try. Where does one start looking?

***

Jim stood at the bus stop racking his brains when his eyes fell upon a mysterious-looking man wearing sunglasses and a turned-up collar. He peered around shiftily as though he didn't want anyone to see him, but Jim had spotted him anyway. "This is my lucky break," he muttered to himself. "That man is just bound to be up to no good."

Luckily, the man was catching the same bus as Jim, so he immediately set to work. Mr Hart had told him that a good detective must never be seen by his enemies. As he got onto the bus and paid his fare, Jim wondered just what the man could be doing. Perhaps he was planning to rob a bank or kidnap someone. No, he was probably plotting a terrible murder. Even better, it could be the mysterious jewellery thief that Percy Caramel had been talking about and Mr Hart had been trying to hunt down for so long. Imagine catching him!

"Well done, James." He could hear Mr Hart's voice quite clearly. *"I knew I could count on you to come through."*

The bus rumbled along the streets when suddenly Jim realised that while he was daydreaming, his suspect was getting off. Jim hastily jumped up and joined the queue to leave. The bus had stopped outside a large jewellers and suspicions were growing in Jim's head, but the man walked straight past the store, so that was that.

What is he up to?

"I mustn't be seen," Jim reminded himself. Out of his briefcase he took a folded-up newspaper that his mother had bought him. The streets were rather busy with lots of shoppers and Jim had a difficult job following the man, especially with a newspaper in front of his face and his glasses constantly sliding down his nose. He did notice though that the man was carrying a large black suitcase that he held very close to his chest.

I bet it's stolen money. Just think! I'm in hot pursuit of a bank robber.

Jim's hopes were rising by the minute. He could just see it all.

> *Detective James Dopeyworth Catches Million Pound Bank Robber*

Just think of that headline in all the newspapers. He would be a hero!

Hang on a minute though, he hadn't caught him yet. All he had to do was prove that the suitcase was full of money. He couldn't very well go up and ask him to open up the case, could he? What if he was wrong?

Jim didn't know what to do. He was so caught up in his own thoughts that he didn't see the lady walking a rather large poodle heading straight towards him.

Crash. Jim tripped right over the lead and lost his balance. He lunged forward, falling headfirst into his suspect, sending them both crashing to the ground.

The suitcase flew through the air and burst right open. Jim's eyes nearly popped out. The case was jam packed full of money, just as he thought it would be!

"Now, sir," said Jim with an air of authority as he cuffed the man with his specially polished Sherlock handcuffs and led him away, "I'm afraid that you are under arrest on a charge of theft."

"Don't be ridiculous," shouted the man as he tried to loosen himself from Jim's firm grasp. "You can't just handcuff me like that. On what grounds, may I ask, am I under arrest?"

Jim smiled to himself as he led him up the steps of the nearby police station. "*Oh, can't I just?* Theft! I am arresting you on grounds of theft!"

By this time, the man was bright red and sweating profusely, and he looked as though he could cheerfully have knocked Jim out.

"Can I help you, sir?" A tall burly-looking officer looked down upon Jim who, by this time, was looking extremely pleased with himself.

"Yes, actually. Detective Dopeyworth at your service. I've brought in this man on suspicion of theft, and I can assure you that I have been in hot pursuit of him all morning."

"Have you anything to say, sir?" said the policeman. "May I warn you that anything you do say may be taken down and used as evidence against you?"

"Yes, I have actually," the red-faced man snapped back. "Get me out of these handcuffs immediately and I will show you EXACTLY who I am."

The policeman turned to Jim and asked him to release the gentleman while he stood guard, but there was a problem... Jim had never used his special Sherlock handcuffs before, and he didn't have a key.

Jim's suspect got madder and madder as Jim tried everything he could think of to release him. He dipped his hands in freezing cold water and pulled and pulled... no luck. He tried to saw the handcuffs with his trusty Swiss army knife... no luck. He even resorted to smearing his hands in butter from the poor policeman's sandwich that he had been saving for his lunch break... still no luck.

What am I going to do? By this point, Jim was getting quite anxious.

There was only one thing for it... They would have to call the fire brigade.

Jim's hand shook as he dialled the number.

"What service would you like, please?" said the operator.

"Errrmm, fire brigade, please," Jim stammered. "I need to free a man from some handcuffs."

Please don't let this go wrong, Jim thought as they waited. His suspect was madder than a wasp. Trying to be a hero was a tough job.

When the fire engine arrived with four fully kitted out firefighters leaping into action, Jim was starting to have serious regrets about his rather impulsive actions.

"What have we got here?" The fire chief smirked at the situation laid out in front of him. "Get out the Master Blade," he called back to his team. "This one looks quite tricky."

The "Master Blade" was a very large saw that was pulled out of the fire engine.

"Stand back, lads," shouted the fire chief. "It's about time we gave this new-fangled equipment a try."

One of the firefighters held the suspect's arms as another beavered away with the saw. Sparks were flying everywhere and the whole commotion had drawn quite a crowd of onlookers.

"Watch my suit, you idiot," the man shouted out as one particularly large spark burnt quite a big hole in his sleeve. "This suit was handmade," he said and, directing his murderous gaze at Jim, added: "I'll be sending *you* the bill." By now, Jim was hoping that the ground would swallow him up.

After what felt like the longest hour of Jim's life and a terrifying few minutes when the Master Blade was sending so many sparks flying that Jim thought the police station might set on fire, his suspect was finally free to reach into his jacket.

"Here... you idiot!" he bellowed as he thrust a shiny black and gold business card into the officer's face.

The policeman immediately turned very pale followed by a fetching shade of red. "I am so terribly sorry, sir," he mumbled. "I had no idea."

The man turned to Jim, his face furious. "As for you, Dopeyworth, I will have you know that my name is Lord Archival, and I am the manager of Worthing and Worthing Bank, the largest bank in England. The suitcase that I was carrying was full of money from a very important client of ours that I was personally depositing in the bank for them... NOT THAT IT IS ANY OF YOUR BUSINESS."

Gulp.

"Oh dear," Jim started to stutter. "I am most sorry."

"It's no good being sorry," Lord Archival bellowed. "My precious time has been wasted. My client's time has been wasted, my suit is ruined, and I am covered in butter!!!! Am I right in thinking that you are from Scotland Yard?"

"Yes, sir." Jim gulped.

"Then you can be sure that your employer will hear of this. Now get out of my sight."

As Jim sat on the bus, the newspaper headline had changed.

Butter Fingers Dopeyworth Catches and Arrests Lord Archival on Suspicion Of Stealing His Own Money

Jim's shoulders dropped. *I've done it again, haven't I? What is Mr Hart going to say now? And worse, what is Mum going to say?*

He had let everyone down. Even the policeman had given him a withering look despite Jim trying his best to put his sandwich back together. *What a silly fool!*

Jim disembarked from the bus a stop early. He needed time to think things through. All of the local children coming out of school smiled at him, but his face felt stiff, stuck in an unhappy frown. He just didn't feel like smiling back even when he noticed a group of children waving to him excitedly from under a huge oak tree and beckoning him over.

"Please, mister." A little girl looked up at Jim with her bright blue eyes full of tears. "There's a kitten stuck up the tree. Will you get it? Please?"

Jim nodded absentmindedly. Surely the day couldn't get any worse, so he might as well help. "Sure. Where is it?"

The little girl clapped her hands together with glee. "Thank you so much. It's up there."

Jim found himself hurried towards the enormous oak tree as the crowd of children chattered excitedly and waited for the big rescue to take place. The kitten was wobbling precariously on one of the top branches. *Stupid thing*, he thought. *Why did it have to choose this tree?*

"Here, kitty kitty." *Please come down*, he prayed. The kitten refused to budge, and a dozen pairs of eyes were upon him, so Jim took a deep breath and started to climb. It was a long way to the top and Jim hadn't climbed a tree since he had been a little boy. This was much harder than he thought.

As Jim slowly reached the top, he stretched out to the trembling creature when it let out a huge yawn before sauntering confidently back to the ground.

On seeing that the kitten was safe, the children lost interest and started to walk away, leaving Jim halfway up the huge tree.

"Thanks a lot," he called out and then heard a very loud ripping sound as he caught his trousers on a sharp branch.

Oh no!!! This just isn't my lucky day.

The kitten sat patiently waiting for Jim as he got down from the tree, so Jim bent down and picked it up. It looked well fed and was wearing a smart collar with a shiny bell, so it must belong to someone. It purred back in appreciation as Jim gently picked it up.

"Well, I guess we better try and find out where you live."

Jim went from door to door around the park with the purring kitten tucked safely under his arm, but nobody seemed to know where it had come from. The more Jim walked, the bigger the hole in his trousers was becoming, and he felt weary after such a long and difficult day.

Okay. Just one more and then I had better call the local vets, Jim thought.

The last house facing straight onto the park was enormous and it looked like it might be occupied by someone rich and important. It was the sort of place that Jim dreamed about having. Somewhere fitting for a world-famous detective.

"I suppose we had better try here. I hope that they have some spare trousers or a needle and thread."

Jim carried the kitten up the winding driveway to what looked like a very imposing shiny black door.

He rang the doorbell and a maid in full uniform answered immediately.

"Is this your kitten?" He thrust the purring kitten towards the maid hopefully. "I found it up that big oak tree in the park."

The maid took the kitten from Jim with a huge smile. "Oh, Suki, you little rascal. Mummy was getting so worried." She turned to Jim. "Thank you so much, sir. Please, come in. Would you like a cup of tea? You look as though you need one."

"Thank you." Jim threw a quick glance at the mirror in the hall as he stepped inside and couldn't help but redden at the sight of himself. He had twigs in his hair, his glasses were crooked, and he had a big blob of soil on the end of his nose.

Suddenly, a very large man stormed through the hallway, making the huge chandelier rattle, and Jim jumped back in surprise, nearly losing his balance in the process. The man had dark, greasy hair and a thunderous expression on his face that made Jim's tummy feel quite unsettled.

Jim opened his mouth to protest when he caught the man briefly smiling at the maid, who turned a fetching shade of pink.

Hmmmm, he looks familiar, Jim thought but couldn't quite remember where he knew him from.

There was something a bit strange going on here! Jim could smell a rat!

"See you soon, Eliza," the man whispered, ignoring Jim as he slammed the door behind him.

Crikey, thought Jim. *He's a bit scary. I wouldn't like to get on the wrong side of him!!*

He followed Eliza through to the parlour and sat down to wait. It was a beautiful room with soft velvet sofas and huge squashy cushions. Jim dusted down his torn pants and settled himself down, knowing that soon he would have to face the music after his terribly embarrassing day. He closed his eyes for a moment and was enjoying the comfort and the quiet when he heard the most ear-piercing scream.

"Aaaaahhhhhhhhhhh!"

Eliza dropped the tray that she was carrying in with a loud *CRASH* and Jim jumped quickly to his feet. They both looked at each other and ran into the next room to find out what could have possibly happened.

A small, perfectly dressed lady stood in front of them. She was white-faced with shock and staring aghast at the family safe.

"My jewels. They are gone, Eliza. All of them. My precious jewels." She looked tearfully at the maid. Then her eyes suddenly fell upon Jim. "Who on earth is this man? Where are my jewels? Have you got them?"

Eliza pushed Jim forward. "He found Suki, Lady Chapelbottom. Isn't that wonderful? I was beginning to think we would never see her again after all this time."

Jim gave a small bow. "Allow me to introduce myself, Lady Chappedbottom."

"Chapelbottom, Chapelbottom, if you please."

Jim reddened at his mistake but continued. "James Dopeyworth, madam. I am a detective from Scotland Yard."

At the word "detective", Lady Chapelbottom perked up. "Detective? Then you couldn't have arrived at a better time. You can help me find my stolen jewels. What do you think?"

Jim didn't know what to say. His mouth suddenly felt very dry, and he longed for the cup of tea that he had been promised. After his mishap this morning, he probably wouldn't be a detective much longer, but his boss had told him to find a mystery to solve by the end of the day… and this was a mystery!

There was only one thing for it. He had to rise to the challenge.

"If you could just wait a few minutes, I will talk to my boss at Scotland Yard and discuss what we are going to do. In the meantime, please do not touch anything and try not to panic. Your problem will soon be solved with Detective Dopeyworth on the case!"

Thirty minutes later, Jim was sitting in Mr Hart's office waiting for him to arrive. His pants were ripped, and he was dripping in sweat as he had run all the way from Lady Chapelbottom's, but this was going to be worth it! He knew that this morning hadn't gone well, but if he just had this one last chance, he could prove to everyone that he wasn't a cloth head after all.

The door to the office was flung open with a huge bang and in strode Mr Hart. Jim's immediate thought was that he looked rather angry and that this may be a good time to make a run for it.

"Dopeyworth, I don't actually believe what I have heard today," he shouted before Jim had a chance to utter a word. "One of my detectives arrested the manager of Worthing and Worthing Bank. He smeared him in butter? He set his suit on fire? As soon as I found out, only *one* name came into my head. *Dopeyworth*."

Mr Hart took a deep, deep breath and with every exhalation said:

"*YOU. ARE. FIRED.*"

Jim turned pale. "Please, Mr Hart," he begged, "just give me one last chance. I've found a mystery to solve. Lady Chapelbottom's family jewels have gone missing, and she has asked me to help her find them. If you would just give me a few more days, I am sure that I could prove to you that I'm not such a bad detective. I promise you I can. The robbery could even be linked to the jewellery thief that you have been searching for. It might be the work of the Green Emerald Gang."

"Dopeyworth," Mr Hart boomed, "no one could convince me that you will ever make a good detective. I can't afford for Scotland Yard's reputation to be damaged. There's the door... Goodbye!!!"

Poor Jim rose to his feet and slunk out, and his shoulders drooped. He was devastated. Once again, his dreams had been shattered. *This is all my fault. I should have never taken this job... I'm just not good enough to be a detective...* Tears rolled down his cheeks and plopped noisily onto the tiled floor. He thought he would be glad that he wasn't a detective anymore, but all he felt was miserable and defeated. What was he going to do?

Jim walked home and quietly let himself in through the front door, hoping that he could avoid his mother, but no such luck.

"Jim, darling, you are home early. How did...?"

Jim raised his hand slowly to wipe away a tear that threatened to roll down his cheek.

"I'm sorry, Mum," he sniffed. "I'm just not good enough. I can't do this anymore."

Mrs Dopeyworth looked up at her son and smiled.

"You will be a wonderful postman. I just know it." And with that she turned and walked quickly into the kitchen but not before letting out a small sob that she had tried very hard to cover up.

Poor Jim turned right back around and headed out. *I've let everyone down again*, he thought. *I'm useless. What am I going to do now?*

As Jim stood outside in the sunshine, he thrust his hands into his pocket and his fingers rested upon his favourite magnifying glass. It was one of his most prized possessions and it reminded him of how much he loved being a detective. It was the first magnifying glass that his father had bought him.

He thought about the last Christmas when his father was still alive. They had loved reading Sherlock books together and playing detective games. Mr Dopeyworth would always help Jim look for mysteries to solve, and Jim loved hearing about the time when his father had worked on a robbery case alongside Sherlock Holmes. He never tired of hearing about how they had uncovered all of the clues that had led them to catching the most elusive robbers in the country, the famous “Blyte Bandits”.

He could almost hear his father’s voice now.

“Don’t give up, son. There is always a way if you just keep looking.”

He could do this. He knew he could. And this time, he wasn’t just going to roll over. He was meant to be a detective, not a postman… He knew it. It was in his blood. This was all he had ever wanted, and he wasn’t going to give in.

Come on, Jim, he thought. *Don’t give up. Remember what Dad used to say.*

He would make his mum and dad proud. He would show old “Sausage Fingers” Hart. He straightened his shoulders and puffed out his chest! This was his case to solve. It was meant to be, and no one could take that away from him. He would find those jewels and then he would be a hero. He would show Mr Hart what a wonderful detective he was and make him sorry he fired him.

He opened the front door and shouted,

"Mother, I'm not going to give in!!"

Mrs Dopeyworth rushed towards him. "That's my boy," she cried.

Detective Dopeyworth was going to conquer the world.

***

Problems Arise

"Well, Lady Chapelbottom. Detective Dopeyworth has come to your rescue."

Jim smiled confidently as he sat drinking tea in the parlour. His mother had suggested that he head right back to Lady Chapelbottom's and start to prepare for business. Preparation was the key to success for any good detective.

"Splendid, Mr… May I call you Jim? And please, feel free to call me Avril." Lady Chapelbottom smiled as a blush crept onto Jim's cheeks. "When can you begin?"

Jim thought for a moment as he sipped his tea and nibbled on a chocolate digestive. It was important that he got this right, and he didn't want to make any hasty decisions or silly mistakes. He needed time to think and get ready.

"Tomorrow morning, Lady… I mean, Avril." Jim stood up to leave. "Now, I really must go as I have a lot of preparation to do."

Eliza showed Jim out, and as he made his way down the path towards the road, Jim noticed the large, greasy-haired man from earlier lurking behind the bus shelter. He glanced at Jim for a moment and then turned away quickly.

How strange, thought Jim, looking back at the house where Eliza still stood in the doorway. He waved, but Eliza hastily closed the door.

That's odd. I'm sure that she saw me waving.

As Jim walked the short journey home, his head was literally bursting with excitement. Just think, he had a real mystery to solve. This wasn't going to go wrong; he could just feel it in his bones. His mother would be so excited when he told her. His dream of being a detective was going to come true. Finally!

Jim opened the door to his home on Sherlockton Avenue and placed his briefcase in its usual space in the hallway. He would act very calmly as though it was just one of those things. He strolled casually into the lounge, but try as he might, he just couldn't conceal his excitement.

"Mother, Mother, I've got a real mystery to solve, a real life mystery."

Mrs Dopeyworth jumped to her feet and hugged him. "Oh darling, that's just so wonderful. Your father would be so proud."

All that evening Jim and his mother sat and talked. Mrs Dopeyworth polished all of Jim's best magnifying glasses and ironed his special spying newspapers with the holes in. They even found the key to his Sherlock handcuffs which Jim carefully threaded onto a chain to put around his neck. He wasn't going to make that mistake again.

When Jim finally retired to bed he just couldn't sleep. He was so excited. It was like a dream come true. A mystery to solve. His big moment to make everyone proud. He closed his eyes and finally drifted into a dream where a cat called Suki was chasing the manager of a very famous bank with Jim in hot pursuit of them both wearing his very best duck pyjamas and carrying a big tub of butter.

***

The next morning, Jim rose bright and early. He was raring to go!

This is it. Jim hugged himself with excitement. *Today, I start a brand new adventure.* He had decided last night that the first thing he was going to do was search the house. He would take all of the family's fingerprints and then go over the house looking for different prints. Maybe the burglar's? Jim thought he had it all worked out. Nothing would stop him now.

"Jim, breakfast is ready," his mother's voice rang out. "Come and get it while it's hot."

Mrs Dopeyworth was already sat at the breakfast table, nibbling on a piece of toast, but in Jim's place was a plate piled high with several rashers of bacon, eggs, sausages and fried mushrooms.

“Mother,” Jim groaned, “how on earth do you expect me to eat all of that?”

Mrs Dopeyworth just smiled at her son. “James, darling, of course you can. A detective can’t go to work on an empty stomach. Now, eat it all up like a good boy.”

Typical.

About 30 minutes later, Jim wiped the remains of his three eggs with his final piece of buttered toast. He patted his rather round tummy as he scraped back his chair to stand up and loosened his belt a notch.

It was time to make a start. Jim had a lot of work to do today. He had agreed to be at Lady Chapelbottom's at 9 o'clock sharp, and it was already 8.30. He gathered all his equipment together and strode out into the sunshine.

"Goodbye, Mother," he called as he closed the door behind him. *Wish me luck.*

Jim strode down the road to Lady Chapelbottom's house. It was only a 10-minute walk from Sherlockton Avenue, and it was a beautiful sunny day. Jim smiled to himself at what a difference 24 hours could make. What a beautiful day to solve a mystery.

As Jim turned the corner onto Lady Chapelbottom's drive, however, his good mood vanished and his heart sank. Parked in front of the house was Mr Hart's car. Jim gazed at it in dismay. Mr Hart, as usual, would try and take over the whole thing and he wouldn't get a look in. Well, he wasn't having it. Not anymore.

He straightened his shoulders and took a deep breath.

"Jim, Jim!" Lady Chapelbottom rushed out of the house and grabbed his arm. "Thank goodness you are here."

"Hello, Avril," Jim replied. "I see that you have visitors?"

Jim followed Avril into the parlour where Mr Hart stood looking rather angry.

"Oh, so it's YOU, Dopeyworth? I might have guessed." Mr Hart glared at Jim. "You can't go taking business off our hands."

Jim tried to look a lot braver than he felt.

"This is *my* case." He turned to face Mr Hart. "Lady Chapelbottom has asked *me* to help her and that is EXACTLY what I am going to do. Isn't that right, Avril??"

"It certainly is." Lady Chapelbottom looked adoringly at Jim. "I do not wish for any other detective but Jim to look for my precious jewels. Eliza will show you out, Mr Hart."

"Lady Chapelbottom..." Mr Hart was getting redder by the minute. "I have seen Dopeyworth at work and I can assure you that he couldn't find those jewels if they were right under his nose."

"Thank you, Mr Hart, but I will be the judge of that. Good day to you."

Mr Hart picked up his hat and turned to leave but stopped to look back at Jim before he closed the door.

"You haven't heard the last of this, Dopeyworth."

Jim sat down in the chair, his knees shaking. Mr Hart could get him into all sorts of trouble if he wanted to, and trouble was the last thing that Jim needed. Still, he needed to do the job he came for and that was exactly what he was going to do.

"Now then, Avril." Jim hoped that his voice wasn't wobbling too much. "First, I would like to start by searching the house. Is that alright?"

Avril was gazing at Jim with starry eyes. "You are so brave," she said, "not letting that nasty man upset you." She sat, her eyes fixed on Jim and a dreamy look on her face.

"I think I'll start in the other room."

As Jim stepped out into the hallway, Eliza jumped away from the door and then continued to dust the chandelier rather furiously.

"Everything okay, Eliza?" Jim was slightly concerned about her jumpy behaviour, but she simply nodded and carried on with her work.

The room next door turned out to be an enormous dining room, the likes of which Jim had never seen before. It was so grand.

"Gracious," Jim exclaimed. "Where do I start?"

Jim reached into his bag for his *Sherlock Holmes Book of Good Advice*. He flicked through the well-thumbed pages until he came across the chapter *Searching Rooms*. "First," he read, "check for loose panels."

Jim started at one end of the room and started to tap each individual oak panel. Round and round the room he went, tap, tap, tap, but every panel seemed just fine. Jim scratched his head as he walked across the room back to the door when he suddenly realised that one of the floorboards creaked quite noisily. Jim bent down and lifted it up.

"Jim, dear?"

It was Avril. Jim quickly put the loose floorboard back. He was sure that Avril wouldn't approve of her beautiful dining room floor being ripped up.

"Jim, why are you sitting on the floor?" Avril exclaimed. "Would you like a nice cup of tea?"

"Yes, please, Avril." *Anything to get her out of the room*, Jim thought.

As soon as Lady Chapelbottom was out of earshot, Jim carefully lifted up the floorboard and let out a small gasp as there, nestled in the void below, laid a large wooden box.

"The jewels," Jim exclaimed as he gingerly lifted the lid up to find a black silk cloth wrapped around something quite big and heavy. Jim carefully lifted it out, but instead of a box of jewels, there was... a *BIG BLACK GUN* and a note:

> *Lady C's bedroom, second on the left. She will be getting ready for dinner at 7.30 pm. Gun preloaded. Archie will be waiting. Good luck.*

Jim's hands shook as he read the note. This was more of a mystery than he had expected. Avril's life was obviously in danger. He hurriedly replaced the box and peeled off his white detective gloves. He didn't want Avril to know. Not yet anyway. She would be too frightened.

And who on earth was Archie?

Jim was just patting down the loose floorboard when a high-pitched shriek rang out. It was so loud that Jim had to cover his ears.

What an earth had happened now?

Was he too late? Was there another gun hidden somewhere else? Was Lady Chapelbottom dead even before he had started?

Jim rushed into the kitchen where Avril stood frantically waving a diamond necklace and a Bourbon biscuit.

Phew.

"Jim, you will never believe what has happened. I have found the jewels in the biscuit tin. Jim, are you listening?"

Jim smiled even though his ears were still ringing. "That's great, Avril, but how on earth did they end up there?"

Avril took a large bite of biscuit to steady her nerves and spluttered through mouthfuls of chocolate crumbs.

"Well, yesterday my brother Brutus came over while I was cleaning the jewels. I didn't want him to see them because he's a nasty piece of work, always after my money. Anyway, I put the jewels in the biscuit tin for safety and I totally forgot that they were there, under the custard creams. What am I like?"

So that was Brutus I saw yesterday, thought Jim. *Hmmmmmmm.*

Avril continued chattering away. "I don't know why Brutus came around though. He never wants to see me unless he needs something. Oh, but poor Jim, you haven't got a mystery to solve now. I am so sorry."

Jim rose hurriedly to his feet. "Never mind, Avril. I'm just glad the jewels have been found. I am sure something else will turn up. I must go."

Avril tugged at Jim's sleeve. "Can't you stay for dinner, Jim? I get so lonely."

"I really must go." Jim was already backing himself out of the door, anxious to get some space to decide what to do. "I have a terrible lot of work to do." He rushed out of the door before Avril could stop him, muttering a hasty "Farewell" as he fled down the path.

It was a very troubled Jim who headed back to Sherlockton Avenue. It was all very well looking for lost jewels, but murder was another thing. Who could have put the gun there? Who would dislike Avril enough to do such a wicked thing?

Poor Jim was in a terrible mess. If he had been a bit more intelligent, he would have removed the box with the gun in, but Jim wasn't very bright sometimes. He just didn't think of things like that. He didn't even think that he had actually left Avril in terrible danger!

By the time Jim got home, it was late afternoon, and for once, he was desperate to talk to his mother. She would know just what to do.

He sat her down and told her exactly what had happened and how he had found the gun and the note.

"Oh darling, how wonderful." Jim was slightly confused by Mrs Dopeyworth's reaction. "Just think, you will have to go straight back to Lady Chapelbottom's.

"I'll what?" Jim spluttered, spraying tea over his best shirt.

"You will have to go now. A note like that could easily be found if it's left any longer." Mrs Dopeyworth glanced anxiously at her watch.

"Mother, I just can't. I would never be able to solve a murder case."

Jim's mother crossed the room to where he was sitting.

"Now listen to me, James Dopeyworth. This is something that you must do. Lady Chapelbottom might die if you don't. It's either that or you ring Mr Hart at once. She is in grave danger." For extra effect, Mrs Dopeyworth tapped her wristwatch sharply! "The note said 7.30 pm. You haven't got long."

Jim sat and mulled over his mother's words. There was no way he was ringing Mr Hart. Once again, his chance had come to be a hero. Surely this time it would work. He would give it one last chance.

"I'll do it," he whispered and then louder: "I'll do it." He hoped that he sounded braver than he felt.

"Who is trying to hurt Lady Chapelbottom?" Jim wondered out loud.

Was it her brother trying to steal her money or the mysterious Archie? Maybe the Green Emerald Gang were involved? It must be someone that knows the house, as they knew where Lady Chapelbottom's bedroom was.

"Why, of course!" Jim thought out loud "That's it!"

"What is, dear?" his mother asked.

Jim suddenly felt quite excited. He was onto something.

"I need to hurry. I am certain I know who it is."

"Oh darling." Mrs Dopeyworth reached forward and hugged her son. "You are so clever. I know you can do this!! I will drive you there. There's no time to waste."

As Mrs Dopeyworth backed her ancient car out of the drive, Jim immediately started to think it would be a lot easier to walk even though the bright sunshine earlier had given way to a huge thunderstorm.

"Mother, you can drive a bit faster, you know," Jim urged as they crawled along the high street. "Mother, it's left here, not right."

Round and round in circles they went as time ticked on. It was difficult to see due to the heavy rain battering the windscreen and every traffic light seemed to be on red. A pigeon suddenly flew out in front of the windscreen and Mrs Dopeyworth's arm shot out to protect her precious boy!

"Mother, for goodness sake," Jim gasped with frustration. "We need to hurry."

As they rounded the corner to Lady Chapelbottom's, Jim noticed a very grand-looking Rolls Royce parked up behind the hedge at the bottom of the drive.

"Just park behind that car, Mother, but please be careful. We mustn't be seen."

Crash. Too late. In her excitement, Mrs Dopeyworth had finally put her foot down and driven straight into the back of the Rolls Royce.

Oops.

That will just have to wait, thought Jim.

"Mother, stay here. I will deal with that later. Please, don't move."

As Jim tiptoed up the drive to Avril's house, Jim's tummy felt quite unsettled.

One thing Jim knew for certain though was that Avril mustn't get wind of what was happening. She was bound to panic and mess everything up. He would have to get into the house and hide somewhere so she couldn't find him.

As Jim approached the front door, he looked around for an alternative way to get in. One of the upstairs windows was slightly ajar, so there was only one thing for it. Time was running out. Avril was in danger, and he had to hurry.

Jim took a deep breath and tried to climb, but the wall was smooth and there was nothing to grab onto. "This is impossible," Jim muttered. "I must find another way." The clock was ticking. It was nearly half past seven. Would he make it?

A little way from the window was a drainpipe. Jim wasn't sure if he would be able to reach the window from the pipe, but he was running out of options. He glanced quickly at his watch: 7.27 pm. Jim prayed he wasn't too late.

Slowly, Jim shimmied up the slippery drainpipe. It was a long way up, but finally he reached the same height as the window. Jim clung on for dear life and started shivering. It was cold and his teeth were chattering. The window looked like a big stretch from where he was, and he was scared of heights.

Bang... All of a sudden, a gunshot rang out from inside the house followed by a blood-curdling scream.

Was he too late? Was Avril dead?

Jim's heart beat faster and faster. He was so terrified he couldn't get down.

"Pull yourself together, Dopeyworth," he scolded himself. "You're a man, not a mouse." Jim gritted his teeth and gingerly reached out one of his feet.

"What an earth are you up to, Dopeyworth?" thundered a familiar voice behind Jim's back.

At the sound of the voice, Jim whipped round with such might that he slid down the pipe a bit and nearly fell. Mr Hart hurried over. His face was redder than a tomato. Jim had never seen him look so furious.

"Get down from that stupid pipe at once. I command it!" But Jim ignored him. He took a deep breath, and with all his might, he pulled himself back up. He was nearly there. Old "Sausage Fingers" wasn't going to boss him about.

He was inches away from the window and the rain was pouring down. Everything was becoming so slippy.

"Come on, Jim, you can do this," he told himself. "Just reach out. You are nearly there."

Jim gingerly stretched out his arm to the open window when disaster struck. His foot slipped and he lurched backwards, just managing to grab the pipe in time. His weight pulled on the pipe and loosened it from the wall. Underneath him, he could see Mr Hart waving furiously. Heading towards them both was the dark-haired man, gun pointing, a big bag under his arm. Everything seemed to be happening in slow motion. Jim heard the click of a gun behind his back. The bracket snapped and Jim felt himself falling backwards.

Crash. Bang!!!

Bright stars were spinning around Jim's head like a merry-go-round and then the world went dark.

***

A few minutes had passed, and Jim's eyes started to flicker open. Where on earth was he? He felt very confused and closed his eyes again.

"Jim, darling." His mother sighed with relief. "Thank goodness you are alright." Jim forced his eyes wide open, only to find Avril and his mother knelt at his side peering down at him anxiously. Mr Hart stood meekly at Avril's side. For once, he seemed lost for words.

"What happened?" Jim's head was spinning around as he struggled to sit up.

"Oh Jim, you have been so brave. My nasty brother Brutus came here with every intention of shooting me. He went into my bedroom thinking I was there, but Eliza had gone in to open the window and he shot her in the leg by mistake as it was dark. Anyway, Brutus tried to escape and was going to shoot Mr Hart, but my brave Jim jumped on top of him from the window and knocked him out. The police have got him now. Jim, you are a hero."

Jim smiled modestly... "It was nothing," he mumbled and with that, he fainted.

The next morning when Jim awoke, he was in his own bed wondering if it had all been a dream until his mother burst through the bedroom door.

"Jim. You're awake. Oh Jim, we brought you home last night and put you straight to bed. You were out cold. You won't believe what happened. Oh, I'm so proud. I still keep pinching myself."

Jim rubbed his eyes and sat up in bed. "Am I a hero now?" he whispered.

"A hero!!" His mother laughed. "You're a celebrity. After the police arrested Brutus, they found sackfuls of missing jewellery at his house, and while you were catching Brutus, I was talking to the man in the Rolls Royce that I bumped into. He was so angry, Jim, and so eager to get away, but he couldn't start his car. It was Lord Archival, Jim. You were right all along. He is part of the Green Emerald Gang that you were talking about. Lord Archival, Brutus and Eliza were all in it together."

Jim could hardly believe what he was hearing. So THAT was who Archie was. They must have been selling the jewels and depositing the money in his bank.

"There are at least eight reporters outside who won't go until they have interviewed you," Mrs Dopeyworth continued. "And Lady Chapelbottom wants to throw a party in your honour tonight. You've got a busy day ahead, dear."

Jim wasted no time. He was up, showered and dressed in 10 minutes. Apart from a few minor bruises and a lump like an egg on his head, he had survived his fall from the night before and felt on top of the world.

Jim hastily combed his hair and puffed out his chest as he gazed proudly at his reflection in the mirror.

"I'm a hero," he kept whispering to himself. "I'm finally a hero."

"James, dear," his mother called out, interrupting Jim's thoughts, "Mr Hart is on the phone."

Jim rushed to pick up the receiver. His heart was thumping so loudly he could hear it in his ears. *What does he want now?*

"James, old chap, Hart here," his boss boomed. "Look, sorry about yesterday. All is forgiven and perhaps I was a bit hasty. I rather need you today. How about it?"

What a cheek, he thought, *thinking I will just go running back when he wants me to.* Jim stood up straight. A new Jim. Confident and assured.

"Sorry, Hart. I've got private business to attend to. Goodbye."

And with that Jim replaced the receiver. *That will show him. Hah!*

The day passed in a whirlwind for Jim. Photographers lined up to take pictures for the papers. Reporters wanted interviews. The police wanted statements. Jim was even on television, much to the delight of his very proud mother. Mr Hart pleaded with Jim to come back to Scotland Yard, but Jim's mind was made up. He was now *Private Detective Dopeyworth*.

It was way past midnight when Jim finally put his favourite duck pyjamas on and climbed into bed.

As he pulled up the cover to his chin, he looked over at the photograph on his bedside table. In a polished silver frame was a picture of his beloved father and Sherlock Holmes standing side by side. Jim smiled as he closed his eyes.

"I did it, didn't I?" he whispered. "I hope that I made you both proud?"

And with that, Private Detective Dopeyworth closed his eyes and dreamed of the adventures that were to come.

The End

Lightning Source UK Ltd.
Milton Keynes UK
UKHW052037241022
411007UK00001B/8